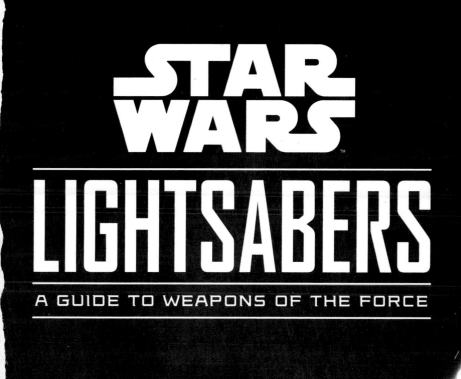

STAR WARS

LIGHTSABERS

A GUIDE TO WEAPONS OF THE FORCE

By Pablo Hidalgo

Brimming with creative inspiration, how-to projects, and useful information to enrich your everyday life, Quarto Knows is a favorite destination for those pursuing their interests and passions. Visit our site and dig deeper with our books into your area of interest: Quarto Creates, Quarto Cooks, Quarto Homes, Quarto Lives, Quarto Drives, Quarto Explores, Quarto Gifts, or Quarto Kids.

Inspiring | Educating | Creating | Entertaining

Disney · LUCASFILM

Published in 2018 by becker&mayer! kids, an imprint of The Quarto Group, 11120 NE 33rd Place, Suite 201, Bellevue, WA 98004 USA.
www.QuartoKnows.com

becker&mayer! kids titles are also available at discount for retail, wholesale, promotional, and bulk purchase. For details, contact the Special Sales Manager by email at specialsales@quarto.com or by mail at The Quarto Group, Attn: Special Sales Manager, 401 Second Avenue North, Suite 310, Minneapolis, MN 55401 USA.

17 18 19 20 21   5 4 3 2 1

ISBN: 978-0-7603-5540-4

Written by Pablo Hidalgo
Edited by Delia Greve
Designed by Sam Dawson
Production management by Tom Miller
Illustrations: page 5, Chris Trevas; page 6, Chris Reiff.

Printed, manufactured, and assembled in China, 01/18.

Design Elements used throughout: metal background ©phiseksit/ Shutterstock

301178

AN ELEGANT WEAPON

With the press of a button, the cylinder-shaped metal hilt releases a brilliant shaft of energy in a sizzling *snap-hiss*. Stopping about a meter from the dish-like emitter, the humming beam of energy appears as a solid, bright core of light radiating a haze of color.

No weapon is more recognizable as a symbol of the Jedi Order than the lightsaber. For over a thousand generations, Jedi Knights carried these elegant blades in their quest to protect peace and justice in the Galactic Republic. The Sith, a dark offshoot of the Jedi, also wield lightsabers. However, in the hands of a Sith, a lightsaber is used for attack, domination, and execution rather than for defense. Only a Jedi Knight can wield a lightsaber to its full potential.

A BRIEF HISTORY

Much of the history of the Jedi Order is shrouded by age and mystery. According to ancient Jedi texts, the Order began on the remote world of Ahch-To before spreading out to protect the early Republic. Historians believe the Jedi have carried lightsabers since their earliest days—when Jedi scholars found a way to bond with the living kyber crystals scattered across the galaxy and transform the crystals' energy-binding abilities into a brilliant blade.

The lightsaber has changed little through the ages, but variations on the design do exist, having evolved to meet specific needs in the long history of conflict in the galaxy.

ANATOMY OF A LIGHTSABER

Lightsaber handles, or hilts, are usually about 30 centimeters long—although some hilts are longer and some are less than half this length. Whatever they may look like on the outside, most lightsabers contain the same technology inside.

The **energy cell (1)** unleashes its power through a Force-bonded **kyber crystal (2)**. When building a lightsaber, a Jedi must use the Force to carefully line up the energy cell with the crystal. A true lightsaber cannot be assembled by a machine. Only those sensitive to the Force can construct one.

A **focusing array (3)** concentrates the released energy into a beam. The kyber crystal gives the beam its color and its unique "feel"— characteristics that determine how it moves and vibrates.

Once the energy is focused, it leaves the handle from a positively charged **energy lens (4)** inside the **blade emitter (5)**. The beam is trapped inside an energy field created by the kyber crystal, which bends the beam back towards a negatively charged high-energy flux aperture in the emitter. To an observer, it looks like the blade simply stops growing, but this loop of energy creates the lightsaber's distinctive hum as well as the spinning effect in the blade's movements, making the weapon difficult to control for those without training.

As the beam, or blade, loops back into the handle, a **superconductor (6)** channels the energy back to the power cell. As a result, a lightsaber is extremely energy efficient; it uses all of its power at once and yet never loses any.

Kyber crystals are rare gems found throughout the galaxy and are valued for their remarkable energy-magnification qualities. For the Jedi, the crystals are unique life-forms that exhibit a presence in the Force. Only through a specific act of attunement— reached through Force-meditation—can a crystal be made ready to use in a lightsaber.

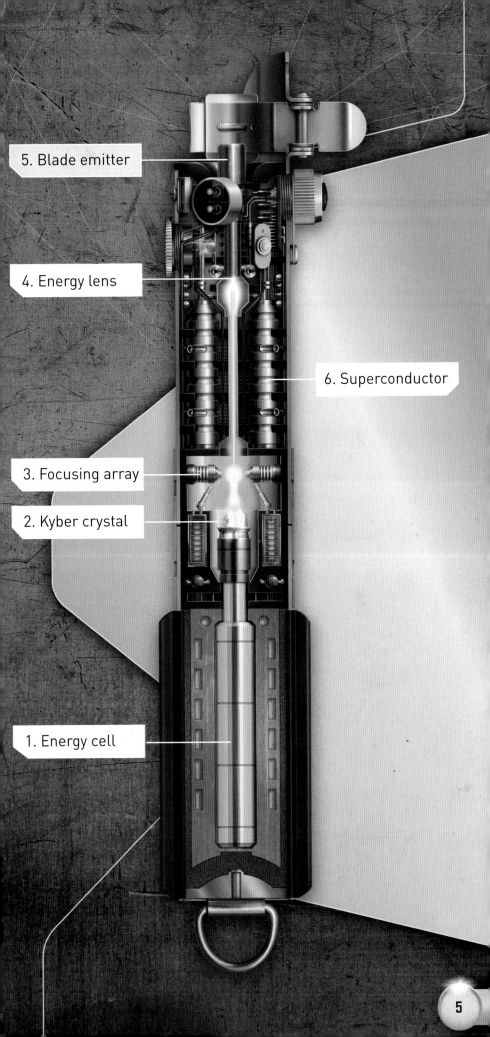

5. Blade emitter

4. Energy lens

6. Superconductor

3. Focusing array

2. Kyber crystal

1. Energy cell

BUILDING A LIGHTSABER

As part of Jedi tradition, each youngling must construct his or her own weapon during training. This begins with a sacred ritual called the *Gathering*, wherein a youngling finds and bonds with the kyber shard that will become the primary crystal of the weapon. Then, the youngling uses the Force to assemble their selected components and technology to contain the crystal.

THE GATHERING

During the time of the Republic, classes, or clans, of younglings would journey to the frigid world of Ilum, home to a rich trove of kyber crystals.

For a youngling, it is not just a matter of finding a kyber crystal but finding the *right* kyber crystal. A crystal will call to the youngling, a call that can only be heard during moments of concentration and clarity. It is this crystal that a youngling can then attune to the Force through a bond. This attunement evokes a color change in the crystal, usually from clear to green or blue, but in some rare cases, purple.

ASSEMBLY AND TUNING

A youngling forges the connection between the crystal and the lightsaber's power source through direct concentration of the Force. In doing so, a Jedi enters a trance-like state, feeling deeply and responding to the unique call of the crystal.

A lightsaber is an extension of a Jedi's Force awareness. Because Jedi let the Force guide their selection of the crystal, the vibration the crystal creates in the lightsaber blade helps Jedi center themselves and find balance in the Force. In this way, a Jedi can center his or her attention beyond the distractions of combat.

EXOTIC LIGHTSABERS

- The **shoto** is a more compact version of a lightsaber with a shorter blade, used primarily as a defensive guard by those who carry two lightsabers.

- A **guard shoto** is attached to a regular lightsaber hilt at a 90-degree angle, allowing the blade to be held parallel to the forearm and spun in a complex form of defense or attack.

- The **dual-phase lightsaber** contains multiple crystals that allow its blade length to be extended or shortened mid-combat.

- A Jedi Temple guard lightsaber is a weapon assigned to those who were tasked with the security of the Jedi Temple on Coruscant. Unlike the traditional Jedi lightsaber, these double-bladed weapons were not personally bonded to the user and were instead simply assigned in order to make those on guard duty as anonymous as possible.

- An Inquisitor lightsaber is a rare design found only in the ranks of a now defunct Jedi-hunting Imperial organization. This double-bladed lightsaber has emitters that sit on a rotating outer ring. Thus the blades emitted from the ring spin at deadly speeds using a frictionless repulsorlift propeller.

INQUISITTOR LIGHTSABER

SITH SABERS

A Sith lightsaber is constructed using similar methods, but the underlying philosophy is quite different. A Sith cannot establish the mutual bond with a kyber crystal like a Jedi does, for the hate, fear, and other dark emotions that cloud a Sith's concentration prevent it. Instead, a Sith imposes his or her angry will onto a crystal, "bleeding" it, which turns the crystal a distinctive red. Some Sith believe the proper method to gain a crystal involves bleeding one captured from a Jedi lightsaber—though in truth, any inert kyber shard can be bled and forcefully weaponized for use in a red-bladed lightsaber.

MYTHS ABOUT LIGHTSABERS

While many galactic citizens know of a lightsaber or "laser sword," few have ever seen one in action. This has led to many misunderstandings about their function.

MYTH:

A lightsaber is powered by the Force.

FACT:

A common energy source, such as a diatium cell, can power a lightsaber. This myth may have been sparked by the seemingly endless power of the lightsaber's tiny power cell or that the Force is used in the construction of the weapon. But in truth, a lightsaber can be charged from a power outlet.

MYTH:

Only a Jedi or Sith can wield a lightsaber.

FACT:

Anyone could pick up a lightsaber and use it, but lightsabers are extremely difficult to wield. Those used to swinging solid swords often find using a weightless blade a challenge—one that can have dangerous consequences. Only through rigorous training and enhanced senses through the Force can a Jedi use a lightsaber to its full potential.

THIS WEAPON IS YOUR LIFE

A Jedi's connection with his or her lightsaber is a powerful bond, but not one of emotional attachment. It takes a lifetime for a Jedi to achieve true mastery of their weapon.

Lightsabers have few moving parts, which makes them quite rugged. They can operate in the frigid temperatures of space or in the scorching heat of a fiery world. Nonetheless, the components of a lightsaber can be susceptible to the elements, and a Jedi must take special care of his or her weapon.

BASIC GUIDELINES

1. Standard lightsabers and water don't mix.

While some protective measures do exist, such as flashback waterseals, igniting a lightsaber underwater can be a problem. The weapon may boil the surrounding water, spinning turbulence and making it difficult to control. Should a Jedi become submerged in water during the course of an assignment, he or she had best make sure the lightsaber is prepared for such a journey.

2. Maintain proper alignment.

Care must be taken to ensure the focusing array of the lightsaber remains in the proper position. A damaged crystal could cause the blade energy to destabilize and the power cell to explode.

3. Guard your lightsaber.

Above all, Jedi must keep track of their lightsabers. Should a lightsaber fall into the hands of an unpracticed or dishonorable person, it will almost always lead to tragedy.

A Jedi who loses a lightsaber often builds another. In times of great need—such as the emergency of the Clone Wars—the Order kept replacement lightsabers for Jedi to use while they built a new one.

OBI-WAN KENOBI

NOTES

Obi-Wan Kenobi built this lightsaber as a Padawan to resemble that of his mentor, Qui-Gon Jinn, as a show of respect. Obi-Wan lost this lightsaber on Naboo when Darth Maul kicked it into a smelting pit. He rebuilt an exact replica that he used until the start of the Clone Wars, when it was taken by the Geonosians. Obi-Wan then created a new design. (See pages 44–45.)

ANALYSIS

1. The blade emitter is not covered or protected; instead, it is a flat projection plate.

2. The scalloped handgrip lets Obi-Wan command a firm grasp of his weapon.

HILT LENGTH:
28.00 centimeters (11.02")

HILT WIDTH:
5.00 centimeters (1.96")

MATERIAL:
Alloy metal

BLADE COLOR:
Blue

ANALYSIS

The ridged handgrip contains a series of micro-power cells, which enables more control over the lightsaber's current charge levels.

HILT LENGTH:
28.50 centimeters (11.22")

HILT WIDTH:
3.80 centimeters (1.50")

MATERIAL:
Alloy metal

BLADE COLOR:
Green

QUI-GON JINN

NOTES

Qui-Gon Jinn's lightsaber may not be as ornate as that of his mentor, Count Dooku, but, true to his rebellious ways, he used it to master the same classical fighting techniques as well as untraditional combat forms from across the galaxy. After Qui-Gon's death, Obi-Wan briefly used this lightsaber to defeat Darth Maul before returning it to the Jedi Temple.

YODA

NOTES

With a small, stooped appearance, Yoda
may not have looked like a great warrior, but
his skills with a lightsaber were unequaled.
Rather than carry his weapon on his belt,
Yoda concealed it within the fabric around
his waist. During his battle with Darth
Sidious, Yoda lost this weapon inside the
massive Galactic Senate chamber.

ANALYSIS

Yoda's lightsaber is small in comparison with the lightsabers of other Jedi. It is similar to a shoto blade used by some specialists.

HILT LENGTH:
15.00 centimeters (5.90")

HILT WIDTH:
2.80 centimeters (1.13")

MATERIAL:
Alloy metal

BLADE COLOR:
Green

NOTES

Darth Maul based the design of his double-bladed lightsaber on ancient plans found deep within a Sith Holocron owned by Darth Sidious. Eager to destroy the Jedi, Darth Maul felt a single-bladed weapon was far too limiting.

DARTH MAUL

ANALYSIS

Functioning as a saberstaff, Darth Maul's weapon consists of two lightsabers fused together so the blades extend in a single line. Each blade can be ignited separately, depending on the situation and the opponent being faced.

HILT LENGTH:
49.50 centimeters (19.50")

HILT WIDTH:
4.40 centimeters (1.75")

MATERIAL:
Alloy metal

BLADE COLOR:
Red

ANALYSIS

This precisely crafted, tapered hilt is covered with a gleaming electrum-plated finish—a decoration allowed only for senior Jedi Council members. Besides its uniquely crafted exterior, this lightsaber is also noted for its purple blade.

HILT LENGTH:
28.00 centimeters (11.02")

HILT WIDTH:
6.35 centimeters (2.50")

MATERIAL:
Electrum-plated alloy

BLADE COLOR:
Purple

MACE WINDU

NOTES

Mace Windu carried several lightsabers in
his long career, but this last one was the
most remarkable. When Mace bonded
with his gathered kyber crystal, it took
on a distinct purple hue—rare, but not
entirely unique in the Order. The midsection
unscrews to allow easy access to the central
crystal chamber. Windu used this lightsaber
to dispatch Jango Fett, creating an enemy in
his son, young Boba Fett.

KI-ADI-MUNDI

NOTES

As a species, Cereans prefer low-tech culture. Though Ki-Adi-Mundi was comfortable with modern technology, he still admired the simpler Cerean ways. He purposely designed his lightsaber hilt without frills or accents. During his meditation, Ki-Adi-Mundi's dual, or binary, brain bonded with two crystals. Thus his lightsaber carries both.

ANALYSIS

The ridges along the upper half of the handle allow for a firm two-handed grip.

HILT LENGTH:
26.60 centimeters (10.47")

HILT WIDTH:
4.50 centimeters (1.77")

MATERIAL:
Durasteel

BLADE COLOR:
Blue or green

ANALYSIS

This rugged lightsaber design is noted for the radiator casing segment, which forms the tapered, or conical, shape at the base of the hilt.

HILT LENGTH:
28.00 centimeters (11.02")

HILT WIDTH:
5.00 centimeters (1.96")

MATERIAL:
Alloy metal

BLADE COLOR:
Blue

PLO KOON

NOTES

A serene Jedi Master, Plo Koon is not one
to brandish his lightsaber without a strong
reason as he prefers to find alternatives to
conflict. But when he is left with no choice,
his commanding voice and brilliant blade
combine to create unparalleled authority.
Master Plo carries a hilt design that is quite
common among Jedi who see themselves as
sentinels.

KIT FISTO

NOTES

Being from an aquatic species native to the waters of Glee Anselm, Kit Fisto modified his lightsaber so the beam could energize even when fully submerged in water. To achieve this, he used two crystals charged by an ignition pulse that is split into two currents. Fisto's customization served him well when he was assigned to such watery battlefronts as Kamino and Mon Cala during the Clone Wars.

ANALYSIS

1. The blade emitter is widened to support twin crystals.

2. Integral flashback waterseals built into the hilt allow this lightsaber to ignite underwater.

HILT LENGTH:
26.60 centimeters (10.47")

HILT WIDTH:
3.80 centimeters (1.50")

MATERIAL:
Alloy metal

BLADE COLOR:
Green

1

2

ANALYSIS

The elegant curved handle design, along with its flourishing blade-emitter guard, makes this lightsaber hilt distinct. It also contains a reserve power cell in its base.

HILT LENGTH:
35.50 centimeters (13.98")

HILT WIDTH:
7.60 centimeters (3.00")

MATERIAL:
Alloy metal

BLADE COLOR:
Red

COUNT DOOKU
(A.K.A. DARTH TYRANUS)

NOTES

This notable design departs from Jedi tradition, but the curved hilt perfectly suited the classic form of lightsaber combat Count Dooku perfected. He transformed the original kyber crystal into a red gem when he reassembled the weapon and took the Sith title Darth Tyranus. Though Dooku turned his back on the Jedi traditions, he still greeted his opponents with the customary salute of a Jedi when engaging in duels.

TRAINING LIGHTSABER

NOTES

Jedi initiates—students who have yet to be paired into Padawan-Master relationships—begin training with lightsabers at a very young age: three or four years old for humans. Training lightsabers emit low-intensity blades that cannot cut and are not lethal. Contact with a training blade will only sting or numb an opponent; however, these blades do convey an accurate sensation of holding a real lightsaber.

ANALYSIS

Training lightsabers are smaller than standard lightsabers, built for the small hands of Jedi initiates.

HILT LENGTH:
Varies, but typically
16.50 centimeters (6.50")

HILT WIDTH:
Varies, but typically
2.50 centimeters (1.00")

MATERIAL:
Durasteel, copper, and tempered plastics

BLADE COLOR:
Blue or green

ANALYSIS

Like that of Plo Koon's lightsaber, this hilt features a conical radiator casing segment at the base. However, this hilt includes a manganese brass casing at the base—a treatment that prevents corrosion.

HILT LENGTH:
28.00 centimeters (11.02")

HILT WIDTH:
5.00 centimeters (1.96")

MATERIAL:
Alloy metal

BLADE COLOR:
Green

LUMINARA UNDULI

NOTES

A serious-minded Jedi Master, Luminara studied many Jedi traditions and was inspired to mold her lightsaber after that of one of the greatest Jedi warriors. Luminara's Mirialan heritage made her incredibly agile and flexible—qualities she used to the fullest when engaging in lightsaber combat.

ANAKIN SKYWALKER

NOTES

Anakin Skywalker had visions of the dark side while in his trance-like state in the sacred caverns of Ilum, where he meditated on the construction of this lightsaber. The weapon is in contrast to the delicate saber design of his mentor, Obi-Wan Kenobi. Anakin built his lightsaber instead for maximum power. However, he lost this lightsaber just prior to the Clone Wars when factory equipment on Geonosis cut the handle in two.

PABLO-JILL

Grievous claimed Pablo-Jill's lightsaber from floating debris, after Grievous injured him during an intense duel in a collapsing satellite city over Duro.

EETH KOTH

Koth lost his lightsaber to General Grievous when the Separatist warlord captured him in the Saleucami system.

ANALYSIS

The thick cylinder shape along with the contrasting alloy and carbon gives this lightsaber a blunt, imposing profile.

HILT LENGTH:
28.00 centimeters (11.02")

HILT WIDTH:
5.00 centimeters (1.96")

MATERIAL:
Alloy metal and carbon composites

BLADE COLOR:
Blue

NOTES

Generally, someone incapable of using the Force would find wielding a lightsaber difficult. However, the advanced technology built into Grievous's mechanical body gave him supernaturally fast reflexes and coordination. He could also split his two arms into four, letting him wield four lightsabers at a time.

While Grievous kept a grim trophy room in his hidden lair and carried many stolen lightsabers in the lining of his cape, these four lightsabers were his greatest prizes.

HILT LENGTH:
29.20 centimeters (11.50")

HILT WIDTH:
6.65 centimeters (2.60")

MATERIAL:
Alloy metal

BLADE COLOR:
Blue

HILT LENGTH:
26.60 centimeters (10.55")

HILT WIDTH:
3.80 centimeters (1.50")

MATERIAL:
Alloy metal

BLADE COLOR:
Green

AAYLA SECURA

NOTES

Aayla Secura's extended assignments on frontier worlds with her Master, Quinlan Vos, often kept her far from Coruscant. As such, she chose to construct a functional weapon that allowed for easy maintenance and upkeep. Unable to rely on the resources of the Jedi Temple when in the field, Aayla made do with common tool kits to keep her lightsaber maintained.

RORON COROBB

When General Grievous stormed the Republic capital, he cut through layers of security forces and Jedi protectors, including Corobb. He was killed by Grievous while defending Chancellor Palpatine.

SHAAK TI

As the last line of defense for Chancellor Palpatine, during the final battle of the Clone Wars, Grievous ensnared Shaak Ti with electrified cables, which knocked her unconscious and allowed Grievous to steal her lightsaber.

HILT LENGTH:
26.80 centimeters (10.55")

HILT WIDTH:
4.30 centimeters (1.70")

MATERIAL:
Alloy metal

BLADE COLOR:
Green

HILT LENGTH:
26.60 centimeters (10.55")

HILT WIDTH:
3.30 centimeters (1.30")

MATERIAL:
Copper and durasteel

BLADE COLOR:
Blue

GENERAL GRIEVOUS

ANALYSIS

This hilt is noted as much for its common, simplistic design as it is for the threaded handgrip on the upper half of the handle.

HILT LENGTH:
26.60 centimeters (10.47")

HILT WIDTH:
4.50 centimeters (1.77")

MATERIAL:
Durasteel

BLADE COLOR:
Blue

ANALYSIS

The threaded section at the center of the hilt allows for a balanced grip for those favoring a single-handed fighting style.

HILT LENGTH:
26.60 centimeters (10.47")

HILT WIDTH:
3.30 centimeters (1.30")

MATERIAL:
Durasteel

BLADE COLOR:
Green

ADI GALLIA

NOTES

Adi Gallia is known for her skills as a diplomat, but when the galaxy plunged into open conflict with the Clone Wars, she took up arms to become a battlefield general. Her lightsaber style is acrobatic and makes good use of her limber physique. She was unable to best the Zabrak warrior Savage Opress in lightsaber combat and fell to his raw strength when he gored her with his horns.

SAESEE TIIN

NOTES

Saesee Tiin used a common lightsaber
handle design shared by several of his fellow
Jedi, including Ki-Adi-Mundi and Aayla
Secura. However, Saesee's lightsaber shows
a little less wear than his colleagues'—not
because he was not a warrior, but because
he was an excellent pilot. For many of his
missions, he was behind the controls of
a starfighter rather than in the thick of
personal combat.

ANALYSIS

Like those of other hilts, the ridges along the upper half of this handle support a two-handed style of combat. This hilt also possesses a locking switch to keep the blade active when thrown.

HILT LENGTH:
26.60 centimeters (10.47")

HILT WIDTH:
4.50 centimeters (1.77")

MATERIAL:
Alloy metal

BLADE COLOR:
Green

ANALYSIS

This style of hilt includes a pair of flat adjustment dials. The uppermost dial controls the blade width, while the second dial switches the energy beam between a pair of focusing crystals.

HILT LENGTH:
26.60 centimeters (10.47")

HILT WIDTH:
3.30 centimeters (1.30")

MATERIAL:
Durasteel and brass

BLADE COLOR:
Green and blue

AGEN KOLAR

NOTES

Agen Kolar and his young Padawan learner
Tan Yuster were two of the Jedi who
accompanied Mace Windu on the mission
to Geonosis that sparked the Clone Wars.
Yuster died in combat, overwhelmed by
superbattle droid forces. Kolar salvaged
Yuster's lightsaber and removed the blue
crystal from its handle, eventually adding it
to his own as a secondary blade to honor the
memory of his apprentice.

OBI-WAN KENOBI

NOTES

Obi-Wan Kenobi constructed this lightsaber
after his promotion to the rank of Jedi Master
at the start of the Clone Wars, replacing a
model design that he had used since he was a
Padawan. (See pages 10 –11.) This lightsaber
was also the model from which Luke Skywalker
constructed and designed his lightsaber. The
gleaming metal alloy would eventually become
tarnished from almost two decades of disuse
amid the wastes of Tatooine.

ANALYSIS

The narrow neck along with the ribbing on the handgrip makes this distinctively Obi-Wan's lightsaber.

HILT LENGTH:
29.20 centimeters (11.50")

HILT WIDTH:
5.00 centimeters (1.96")

MATERIAL:
Alloy metal

BLADE COLOR:
Blue

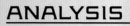

ANALYSIS

This sleek and elegantly designed hilt, composed of valuable metals, is much shorter than most lightsaber handles, which makes it easy to conceal.

HILT LENGTH:
19.00 centimeters (7.48")

HILT WIDTH:
5.00 centimeters (1.96")

MATERIAL:
Aurodium cap with phrik alloy casing

BLADE COLOR:
Red

DARTH SIDIOUS

NOTES

The expense of the metals used to make this lightsaber mattered very little to someone with the wealth and authority of Darth Sidious in his day-to-day disguise as Chancellor Palpatine. Darth Sidious actually constructed at least two of these short-handled weapons. He kept one hidden within a neuranium sculpture in his executive office and another tucked in his sleeve.

SKYWALKER SABER

ANAKIN AND LUKE SKYWALKER, REY

Anakin Skywalker created this lightsaber following the outbreak of the Clone Wars, but Obi-Wan Kenobi took the lightsaber after their battle on Mustafar. Obi-Wan kept the lightsaber while he was in hiding and, a generation later, gave it to Luke Skywalker. Luke lost possession of this lightsaber during his duel with Darth Vader in Cloud City. Decades later, the lightsaber would come into the possession of Rey, a scavenger from Jakku, who brought it back to Luke Skywalker in the hopes he would train her in the ways of the Force, and return to the battle against the dark side.

Anakin Skywalker wielded this lightsaber throughout the Clone Wars, battling countless Separatist droids. It was with this weapon he slew Count Dooku, and also led an assault against the Jedi Temple as Darth Vader.

After Obi-Wan Kenobi defeated Vader on Mustafar, the Jedi retrieved the fallen lightsaber, taking it with him into exile on Tatooine, where he served as young Luke Skywalker's secret guardian.

When Luke was nineteen years old, Obi-Wan Kenobi rescued him from a Tusken Raider attack and brought the young man back to his hut. There, Kenobi passed along the lightsaber as a gift from Luke's father.

Luke lost the lightsaber in a duel with Darth Vader, who wounded Luke by cutting off his hand. The lightsaber then plunged into a deep abyss within the industrial heart of Cloud City.

ANALYSIS

Similar in look to Anakin's first lightsaber (see pages 32–33), this gleaming hilt contains numerous additional technical interfaces, which grew out of Anakin's passion for tinkering with technology and engineering.

HILT LENGTH:
28.00 centimeters (11.02")

HILT WIDTH:
5.00 centimeters (1.96")

MATERIAL:
Alloy metal

BLADE COLOR:
Blue

DARTH VADER

NOTES

Following his crippling defeat by Obi-Wan Kenobi and his painful rebirth as a cybernetically enhanced Sith Lord, Darth Vader was without a weapon. Thus Vader created a hilt similar to that of his former lightsaber but with the characteristic red blade of the dark side. The Emperor had ordered Vader to retrieve a crystal from a fugitive Jedi as part of Sith training.

Reclaimed from Cloud City's mechanical innards, the lightsaber entered the collection of Maz Kanata, a thousand-year old space pirate who lived in a castle on Takodana. Maz acted as a steward of the Jedi relic until she found a worthy recipient.

Though she was at first reluctant to carry the lightsaber that called to her through the Force, Rey used it well in a duel against an injured Kylo Ren on Starkiller Base.

Rey brought the lightsaber to Luke Skywalker, who had exiled himself on Ahch-To. She did not know what to expect, but she didn't think Luke to simply toss the weapon aside.

During a duel with Kylo Ren, the lightsaber became the object of a telekinetic Force struggle between Ren and Rey. The weapon tore in two and was destroyed in an immense blast when its kyber crystal overloaded with energy.

ANALYSIS

Darth Vader's lightsaber resembles the one he carried as Jedi Knight Anakin Skywalker, but this design adds darker, heavier accents along its beam emitter, handgrip, and activation matrix.

HILT LENGTH:
28.00 centimeters (11.02")

HILT WIDTH:
6.30 centimeters (2.48")

MATERIAL:
Alloy metal and carbon composite

BLADE COLOR:
Red

ANALYSIS

Inspired by Obi-Wan Kenobi's second lightsaber, this hilt features a ribbed handgrip and narrow neck.

HILT LENGTH:
28.00 centimeters (11.02")

HILT WIDTH:
5.00 centimeters (1.96")

MATERIAL:
Alloy metals and salvaged materials

BLADE COLOR:
Green

LUKE SKYWALKER

NOTES

After Luke lost both his father's lightsaber
and his hand in battle with Darth Vader, he
constructed a replacement from instructions
found in the abandoned hut of Obi-Wan
Kenobi on Tatooine. Luke's lightsaber
strongly resembles that of his old Jedi
mentor, but the added rings of cycling field
energizers give the lightsaber a stronger,
more reliable blade.

KYLO REN

NOTES

At the heart of Kylo Ren's lightsaber is a cracked kyber crystal, which produces its unstable fiery blade. In many ways, the blade mirrors Kylo Ren's intense and volatile personality. With each deadly swipe, the lightsaber blade leaves a trail of embers. The quillon emitter guards protect Kylo's hands from the crossguard blades.

ANALYSIS

On either side of the main blade emitter are a pair of quillon emitters, that vent excess energy from the overstressed kyber crystal into a pair of smaller crossguard blades.

HILT LENGTH:
29.8 centimeters (11.73")

HILT WIDTH:
14 centimeters (5.51")

MATERIAL:
Heat-hardened industrial alloy

BLADE COLOR:
Fiery red-yellow

LIGHTSABER TECHNIQUES

Whenever possible, Jedi would prefer to outmaneuver or outthink their opponents, rather then rely on the power of the lightsaber. But that is not always possible, and Jedi must know how to use their lightsabers effectively.

DEFLECTING BLASTER FIRE

On the surface, it would seem foolish to bring a bladed weapon to a gunfight. However, the Force allows Jedi to exhibit supernatural reflexes that make it possible for them to block incoming blaster fire. A lightsaber blade is capable of deflecting a blaster bolt, and skilled Jedi can aim blasts back toward their enemies.

LONG-RANGE ATTACK

Most lightsabers incorporate a pressure activation lever that causes it to power down if dropped. They may also have a "lock" switch that keeps the blade active, so a Jedi can throw a lightsaber some distance and guide its path through the Force.

CUTTING THROUGH OBSTACLES

Beyond its use as a weapon or an instrument of meditation, a lightsaber is a practical tool. Given enough time, a lightsaber can cut through most substances. Even shield-rated blast doors will melt after extended exposure to a lightsaber blade, making it nearly impossible to imprison an armed Jedi Knight. Most Jedi will not risk slicing through bulkhead walls or high-energy force fields, though, because cutting into such a powerful source could be explosive.

MYTH:

A lightsaber can cut through anything.

FACT:

The key to creating a solid weapon that can clash with a lightsaber blade is not the metal used in construction but rather the energy the metal conducts. Energy transmitted across a metal blade or polearm can fortify a weapon so it can block a lightsaber blade. The electrostaffs of the MagnaGuard droids or the energized weapons of Supreme Leader Snoke's Praetorian Guards, for example, pose a challenge to even trained lightsaber combatants.

JEDI VS. SITH

This duel marked the first time Jedi and Sith lightsaber blades had crossed in centuries. Darth Maul's leaping assault nearly caught Qui-Gon Jinn off-guard. It was only through extreme focus that Qui-Gon was able to shake off any shock and put up a defense. However, if his escape vessel had not appeared in time, it is likely Qui-Gon would have tired under Darth Maul's relentless attacks.

A PADAWAN'S REVENGE

By separating the team of Obi-Wan Kenobi and Qui-Gon Jinn, Darth Maul was able to target each Jedi separately. He wore down Qui-Gon's defenses and dispatched the Jedi Master with a quick jab to his chest. The act enraged Obi-Wan, who attacked Darth Maul in a rush. Though Obi-Wan's heated assault cut through the Sith Lord's double-ended lightsaber handle, it left him vulnerable to a sudden counterattack. Only by centering himself in the Force did Obi-Wan outleap the Sith Lord and surprise Darth Maul with a swipe through the midsection.

DUEL ON GEONOSIS

Anakin Skywalker and Obi-Wan Kenobi faced Count Dooku in an attempt to stop him from fleeing Geonosis. Dooku's Sith lightning blast briefly knocked out Anakin, allowing the Count to focus on Obi-Wan. Count Dooku's elegant use of Form II combat allowed him to slip past Obi-Wan's defenses and wound him on his arm and leg. Though Anakin recovered and forced Dooku back with a flurry of double-lightsaber strikes, Dooku slashed through Anakin's reckless assault and cut off his arm.

DUEL OF THE MASTERS

With both younger Jedi fallen, Count Dooku seemed victorious. Yoda entered the chamber, however, to challenge the sword master. The two Force warriors attempted to defeat each other with displays of telekinesis and other Force abilities, but they were too evenly matched. They turned to their lightsabers, and, with a masterful display, Yoda dodged Dooku's attacks. Only when Dooku threatened the fallen Jedi was he able to distract Yoda long enough to escape.

REMATCH OVER CORUSCANT

Obi-Wan Kenobi and Anakin Skywalker faced Count Dooku again, this time aboard a Separatist flagship. Familiar with Obi-Wan's fighting style, the Dark Lord once again got the better of him. It was Anakin, at Chancellor Palpatine's command, who sliced through Dooku's hands and mortally wounded him to end the duel.

DARTH SIDIOUS vs. JEDI MASTERS

When Mace Windu led a team of Jedi Masters to apprehend Darth Sidious, none of them expected to face the power of the Sith Lord. His innocent appearance as Chancellor Palpatine, along with an application of a concentrated dark side confusion haze, enabled Darth Sidious to take down Agen Kolar, Kit Fisto, and Saesee Tiin. This left Mace Windu to battle the Sith Lord. Windu nearly overpowered Darth Sidious, forcing him into a corner and holding him at blade point. It was Anakin Skywalker who severed Mace Windu's arm, allowing Darth Sidious to win the fight with a blast of Force lightning.

MASTER vs. APPRENTICE

When it became clear that Anakin was lost to the dark side and had adopted the title Darth Vader, Obi-Wan was left with no option but to confront his former apprentice. Years of fighting side-by-side left these warriors evenly matched, and their exhausting duel crossed the fiery landscape of a Mustafar refinery. It was Anakin's overconfidence, fueled by the dark side, which led to his defeat. A mistimed leap over Obi-Wan allowed him to swiftly cut Anakin, leaving him disabled on the shore of a lava river.

THE CIRCLE IS COMPLETE

A generation later, Obi-Wan Kenobi would face Darth Vader once again. While Vader wanted revenge, Obi-Wan was focused on buying time for his friends—including Luke Skywalker. Their duel was careful and measured compared to their previous meeting. Obi-Wan's movements were slowed by age and lack of practice; Darth Vader—recalling the grievous injuries he suffered during their last encounter—fought his former Master with apprehension, while his cybernetic body reduced his actions. Ultimately, Obi-Wan deliberately dropped his defenses, and Darth Vader cut through him, but the Jedi Master mysteriously vanished into the Force.

A NEW JEDI HOPE

Although he had been only briefly instructed by Yoda, Luke Skywalker showed great ability in the Force during his duel with Darth Vader on Bespin. He had enough strength to challenge Vader, but Luke was far too hasty. The Dark Lord used telekinetic attacks and a shocking revelation to overpower the young Jedi. Darth Vader had already cut off Luke's hand when he crushed Luke's spirit by revealing that he was in fact Luke's father, Anakin Skywalker.

THE FORCE BALANCED

When Luke confronted Darth Vader again, he possessed the clarity and wisdom of a Jedi Knight. He had not set out to conquer but rather to redeem the good in his father. However, Vader, being carefully judged by Darth Sidious, enraged Luke by suggesting he would lure his sister, Leia, to the dark side of the Force. Luke lost his composure and attacked Vader. On the brink of the dark side, Luke let go of his anger. He resisted the Emperor's lure of power and stood by his father. When the Emperor nearly killed Luke with an assault of Sith lightning, Darth Vader saved him by turning against the Sith Lord.

FLEDGLING DEFENSE

In the forests of Starkiller Base, young fugitives Finn and Rey found their path to escape blocked by a vengeful Kylo Ren. Though Kylo stood injured, his side wounded by a powerful shot from Chewbacca's bowcaster, he still had the dark side of the Force at his command. A powerful telekinetic push sent Rey reeling, leaving Finn to face Kylo. Weilding the old Skywalker lightsaber, Finn valiantly stood up to Kylo, but, in the end, the dark side warrior struck him down.

LIGHT vs. DARK

As Kylo Ren tried to call Luke Skywalker's fallen lightsaber into his clutches, he found it instead drawn to Rey's hand. Rey's growing Force abilities had fully awakened within her, and she translated years of defense training with her trusty quarterstaff into effective lightsaber combat technique against Kylo Ren. Rey bested Kylo, whose injuries had left him unbalanced. The crumbling of the landscape surrounding them interrupted their battle before it could come to a decisive end.

AN UNLIKELY ALLIANCE

Believing Kylo Ren could be turned from the darkness, Rey surrendered herself to the First Order flagship *Supremacy* in order to confront him again. In a surprising turn, Kylo and Rey fought side-by-side to fend off eight of Supreme Leader Snoke's highly trained Praetorian Guards, but Rey soon discovered Kylo was not fighting for redemption. He was fighting for conquest. He wanted to rule the First Order. Rey rejected Kylo's invitation to power, and in a struggle to gain control of the old Skywalker lightsaber, Kylo and Rey tore it in two, unleashing an explosive burst of power.